MR. LUNCH
+AKES A
PLANE
RIDE

BY J.otto SEiBoLD and VIVIAN WALSH
ILLUS+RA+ED BY J.otto SEiBoLD

VIKING

**Dedicated
to
Theadora**

VIKING
Published by the Penguin Group
Penguin Books USA Inc., 375 Hudson Street, New York, New York 10014, U.S.A.
Penguin Books Ltd, 27 Wrights Lane, London W8 5TZ, England
Penguin Books Australia Ltd, Ringwood, Victoria, Australia
Penguin Books Canada Ltd, 10 Alcorn Avenue, Toronto, Ontario, Canada M4V 3B2
Penguin Books (N.Z.) Ltd, 182-190 Wairau Road, Auckland 10, New Zealand

Penguin Books Ltd, Registered Offices: Harmondsworth, Middlesex, England

First published in 1993 by Viking, a division of Penguin Books USA Inc.

10 9 8 7 6 5 4 3 2 1
First edition
Copyright © J. Otto Seibold and Vivian Walsh, 1993
All rights reserved

Library of Congress Cataloging-in-Publication Data
Seibold, J. Otto.
Mr. Lunch takes a plane ride / by J. Otto Seibold and Vivian Walsh;
illustrations by J. Otto Seibold.   p.   cm.
Summary: Mr. Lunch, a canine bird-chaser extraordinaire, takes his
first plane ride and finds adventure in the skies.
ISBN 0-670-84775-5
[1. Dogs–Fiction. 2. Air travel–Fiction.] I. Seibold, J. Otto. II. Title.
PZ7.W16893Mr 1993
[E]–dc20 92-41927 CIP AC

Printed in U.S.A.
Set in Times Roman and Arbitrary Bold
The illustrations in this book were created on an Apple Macintosh computer using
Adobe Illustrator software.
Without limiting the rights under copyright reserved above, no part of this publication may
be reproduced, stored in or introduced into a retrieval system, or transmitted, in any form
or by any means (electronic, mechanical, photocopying, recording or otherwise), without the
prior written permission of both the copyright owner and the above publisher of this book.

Mr. Lunch was very good at chasing birds.
In fact, he was a professional.

One morning, a surprise phone call stopped everything at Mr. Lunch's bird-chasing office.

RING. RING.

"Is Mr. Lunch, the expert bird-chaser, there?" asked a voice on the other end.

It was the host of a television show. He invited Mr. Lunch to demonstrate some bird-chasing skills on his program.

Mr. Lunch felt honored and accepted the invitation.

"Fabulous," the television host said, "I'll send you the airplane tickets right away."

Plane tickets! Chasing a bird on TV would be a piece of cake, but Mr. Lunch had never been on a plane before.

This was cause for study. He spent the afternoon looking over his many books, maps, and charts. He always liked to be prepared.

Mr. Lunch thought his passport photo was quite handsome. Too bad he wouldn't need it.

A meeting was called to find a volunteer for the show.
Ambrose stepped forward.

Mr. Lunch and Ambrose needed a little help to
pack just the right things.

BIRDY

HORSE

SQUIRREL

FIREMAN

MONKEY

FOOD

CAT

ANT

MIRROR

PUPPY

LITTLE GIRL

RADIO

And then, most important of all, Mr. Lunch said good-bye
to all of his friends.

RABBIT

SNAKE

BABY

ELEPHANT

WORM

OWL

JOE

TURTLE

FISH

CHAIR

BUTTERFLY

BEAR

Now he was ready to take his trip.

First, they drove through the country...

...and through the city...

...and out to the airport.

The airport was a busy place, full of signs, loud noises, and people in a hurry.

Mr. Lunch remembered from his studies that he'd want a window seat. But before he could even ask, he saw a sign that said DOGS RIDE BELOW. Mr. Lunch, being a dog, would have to ride with the luggage in the bottom of the plane.

The bottom of the plane was a place
never mentioned in Mr. Lunch's books.
It was the part with no windows.
    It was there, as he and Ambrose sat alone
in the dim light, Mr. Lunch realized he
wouldn't see with his own eyes what it looked
like to fly. To be above the trees, the houses,
and the clouds, the way he had heard the
birds describe it.
    All he could see with his own eyes was
luggage. And lots of it. Suitcases, boxes, and
bags. What could be in all these bags?
    After a while Mr. Lunch decided things
would be better if he investigated.

Inside one bag was a cello. It belonged to a woman who played in a symphony. Mr. Lunch plucked at some strings, hoping Ambrose, who was an excellent singer, would chirp in. Ambrose was happy to sing along.

Another suitcase had SCIENTIST written on it. Mr. Lunch was interested in science. He looked inside and found everything he needed to perform an experiment.

A third bag smelled good. It was a chef's bag full of sugar and flour and all sorts of cooking stuff. It even had a chef's hat in it.

Mr. Lunch was enjoying his investigation very much.

Seeing the chef's bag reminded Mr. Lunch that it was his favorite time of day: lunchtime. He unpacked his bone and some birdseed for Ambrose. After eating, it was time for a nap.

When Mr. Lunch woke up, he saw a terrible mess. If anyone else saw this his reputation could be ruined. With little time left he hurried to put things back, but it was hard to remember what went where.

As the captain prepared for landing, Mr. Lunch forgot all
about the bags. He realized that he would soon be on television.

Being a dog, it took Mr. Lunch a while to get a taxi.

Mr. Lunch and Ambrose arrived at the television studio just as the program was beginning.

The television host welcomed Mr. Lunch to his studio and asked him to wait with the other guests.

Mr. Lunch almost barked when he saw what was backstage. There sat the same three bags he had opened on the plane. He didn't feel good about this.

The show began with a musical demonstration by the cello player. Unfortunately, Mr. Lunch had replaced her bow with the chef's cleaver, and the song ended on the first note. BOING!

The scientist was next. He was to reveal his new scientific breakthrough. But instead of his notes he had the cello player's sheet music and he ended up with a singing solution.

The TV show host was worried. Usually his show ran a little more smoothly.

Mr. Lunch could see that the chef was using the scientist's formula instead of a recipe. Just as the final ingredient was added...

...there was a huge explosion.

The audience was stunned. They sat in silence until the smoke cleared. And then they saw it: a scientific supercake! The chef screamed, "MY MASTERPIECE!"

But this was no ordinary scientific supercake. Each piece had a different flavor, and the cake was big enough for every one in the audience to have a slice.

What had seemed so bad, now looked like the baking breakthrough of the century.

Mr. Lunch gave his demonstration and it was thought that he had never chased a bird better.

When Mr. Lunch came home he found bags and bags of fan mail waiting for him. He had no idea that bird-chasing was so popular. He answered every letter with a note and an autographed photo.

thank you,
M. LUNCH

Soon Mr. Lunch was back to what he loved best.